HUMBERT AND THE BULLY FROG

Story by Doris Tomaselli & Carol Paterno
Illustrations by Doris Tomaselli

Afterward by Jackie Muller, LCSW-R, Dynamic Intervention Wellness Solutions
Plus an introduction to The Great Swamp with Judy Kelley-Moberg, educator

---

For my late father, Francis Tomaselli, who so wanted to see this book published.
In memory of his father — my Grandpa Humbert. To Mom (Ruth), for always believing.
To my dear friends and awesome Swamp kayaking buddies—Carol Paterno and Lynn Edling.
~ Doris ~

For Doris and her dad and her dad's dad. For Jan and Tanya, and Justin Goodhart.
~ Carol ~

OUR SINCERE APPRECIATION to: Jackie Muller, Judy Kelley-Moberg, Friends of the Great Swamp,
Jan, Tanya, Millennium Printing, Kathy Mathew – web mistress, and our talented photographers:
Justin P. Goodhart – *justinpgoodhart.com*, Carol Paterno, Ken Luhman, Lynn Edling, and Rick Manger.

Published by Daffodil Press, Pawling, NY • daffodil-press.com // ISBN: 978-1-7323600-2-0
Designed by Empress Creative, Brewster, NY • empresscreative.com // Printed by Arrowhead Printing, Duluth, MN • arrowheadprinting.com

Limited First Edition

Deep in the heart of New York's Great Swamp

Where the north and the south flow divides,

The beaver and heron and turtles all romp;

And a most famous frog resides.

What? You don't know about Humbert?

All the toads tell the tale about Humbert.
You may hear them on a warm summer's night,
Down in the Swamp where the whole thing began
With a bully, a frog, and a fight.

You see...

When the sun sets, the Swamp comes to life.
At the Frog Hop, there's dancing and song.

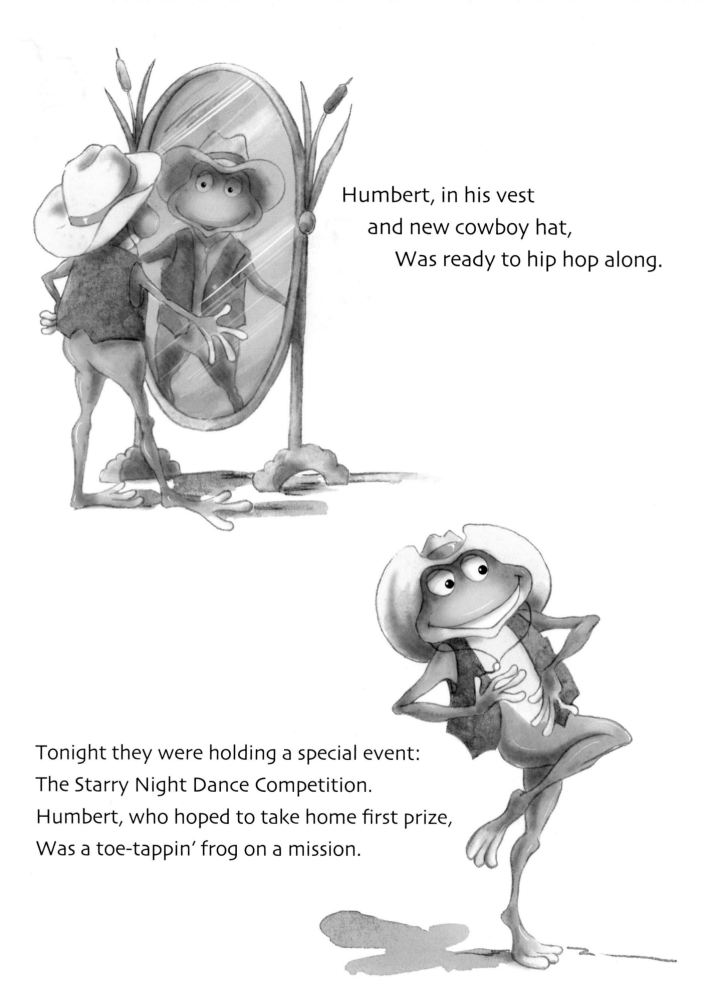

Humbert, in his vest
and new cowboy hat,
Was ready to hip hop along.

Tonight they were holding a special event:
The Starry Night Dance Competition.
Humbert, who hoped to take home first prize,
Was a toe-tappin' frog on a mission.

His partner, a talented dancer,

Was Pollyann Wog — old Wart's daughter.

They'd practiced for weeks, for hours on end,
And when tired, they drank good Swamp water.

They were both feeling ready but nervous,
The contest was about to begin.

Humbert gave Polly a cheering thumbs up.
"We'll do our best hoping we win."

But ...

Down to the bog came Brutus Bullfrog,
Who was mean and ugly and strong, ... *oh no!*
The kind who did whatever he chose
Whether nasty or hurtful or wrong.

Now, Brutus took one look at Polly.
"It's me you'll dance with tonight!"

But Humbert, though frightened,
refused to back down.
Uh-oh!
... Brutus was ready to fight!

The Swamp —
     it got very quiet.

Even the peepers grew still.

The odds were stacked
     against Humbert
          In this showdown
               of muscle and will.

"Oh no!" cried Polly. "He'll smash you!"

But Humbert stood firm for his friend.

"A frog's got to do what a frog's got to do."

"But fighting?" asked Polly. "Is that best in the end?"

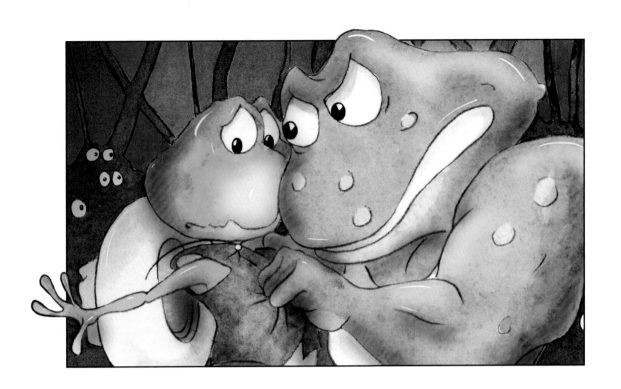

Brutus was a sure bet to beat him,
Humbert knew that he had to depend
Not on fists, but his quick-witted brain,
And a courage within to defend.

So ...

"I-I-I think we should think," stalled Humbert.

"A better duel we can surely devise.

I know! We'll dance! And the last frog left standing

Will be the winner in everyone's eyes."

The Swamp folk all gathered close watching
For the dueling dance to begin.
The crickets then started the music.
At the chorus, the peepers joined in.

Humbert may have been smaller,
But he danced with a song in his heart.

After a while, Brutus grew tired,
And realized he wasn't so smart.

Humbert danced rings 'round that bully.
And Brutus, who had two left feet,

Tripped and — **SPLASH!** — fell into the Swamp
Then admitted that he had been beat.

Polly, smiling, stood by her hero,
As the toads and the frogs cheered, "Hooray!"
Humbert had given a dazzling performance.
His quick thinking saved the day.

So ...

It's clear why they talk about Humbert,
That frog made a bully back down.
Since Brutus was humbled, he's now taking lessons
At a pond on the far side of town.

You see ...

It's not always bigger that's better,
But believing in all you can do.
If courage and brains worked for Humbert the Frog,
Imagine what you can do, too.

Oh! By the way,
Polly and Humbert won!

Do you know a bully?
Did you know The Great Swamp is real? Learn more.

Think like Humbert!
Help for Bullying.

by Jackie Muller, who helps
children work things out

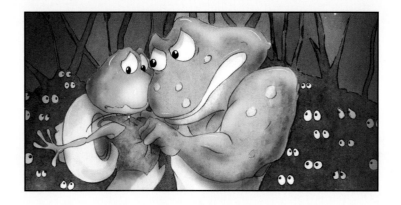

What is bullying?

- Bullying is anything done or said to you that hurts you or makes you feel sad, or scared, or bad about yourself.

How do you know if someone is bullying you?

- If a person says things or does things to you that makes you feel nervous, sad, hurt, or angry.
- It may make you feel like your heart is heavy or your stomach is jumpy.
- You may want to cry, or feel angry or feel like running away. That is all part of how bullying can make you feel.

Why do bully's bully?

- Bullies are sometimes bullied by others and they are hurting inside too so they act out. This is not an excuse.
- Bullies are sometimes embarrassed and look for a way to shift attention off of them and onto another. They think making others feel bad makes them feel or look good. This is not okay.
- Bullies may think they have to be mean to fit in and look cool. They hang out with others who try to be popular with their friends by being mean. This is not okay either.
- Most often bullies only act this way when they have other people around to see. They are looking for attention. This is not the way to get it.
- Bullies think bullying makes them look strong. They just look bad!

Are you being bullied? Here are some things to do.

- Talk to someone you trust, a parent, teacher, or other adult.
- Remind yourself that YOU are the only one who needs to approve of you.

- Ignore them. Bullies can't make you feel bad if you don't let them. And if they see they can't make you feel bad, they may stop.
- Bullies are not better than you. They just want to make you *think* that. But you can be smarter than that!

Are you being a bully? If so, ask yourself why?

- Are people afraid of you? Are people staying away from you? Not inviting you to join them or play with them?
- Are you acting out? Saying or doing mean or hurtful things?
- Are you bullying others because you are bullied too? Are you feeling afraid, hurt or angry?
- Do you bully to fit in with the "popular" kids?

STOP. THINK. ASK.

- Treat others the way you would like them to treat you.
- Talk to someone you trust, a parent, teacher, or other adult. Ask for help. It's a good thing to do. It helps to talk it out. You can learn ways to change, to help yourself, to make good friends and to be happy with who you are and be proud of how you behave.

How did Humbert handle the bully? What can you learn from that?

- Like Humbert, you too can become really good at being smart with a bully. Think before you act. Remember why bullies bully.
- Humbert used the POWER of his mind to think about how to use his own strengths (dancing) to challenge the bully to a better way of handling the situation.
- Can you think of other things Humbert may have done? What would you have done?

REMEMBER: You are AWESOME just the way you are.

• Hang out with people who do not hurt other people. Choose friends who like you for being YOU. You don't have to be "popular" if it means being hurt by someone else or being pushed into hurting others.

What are YOUR strengths?

• A strength is a skill or something that you do well. Like Humbert thinking quickly and believing in his dance skills, he challenged the Bully to a dance off.

REMEMBER: "Think positive" about yourself.

Everyday find something you do that you do well. When you value yourself and know your strengths, you feel good about yourself. And, guess what? A bully can't make you feel bad without you allowing them! So act strong and you will start to feel strong!

There will be times you may be bullied. Most of us have been. You are not alone! If you or someone you know is being bullied, talk to someone you trust, a parent, teacher, or other adult. I'm sure that they will be able to help you and share with you times that they too overcame bullying. Use them and pass that smart thinking on!

The Great Swamp!

JUSTIN P. GOODHART

by Doris Tomaselli
with Judy Kelly-Moberg, educator

Yes! There really *is* a Great Swamp! It is in New York state.

The Great Swamp is a "watershed" area, meaning it provides clean water for people, animals, plants and more.

How does it do that? As the water flows through the Swamp, special minerals in the earth below the water help clean it while wetland plants in and around the water help filter it. (Like brushing, flossing, and rinsing cleans your teeth!)

Clean water is so important. That means people must be smart and care for the Swamp and protect it.

The Great Swamp is big! Thousands of acres of land and the water runs for miles and miles. Water from upland streams and rivers flows through it on its way to the Atlantic Ocean!

If you travel nearby, you will see these signs along the roadside. ➤

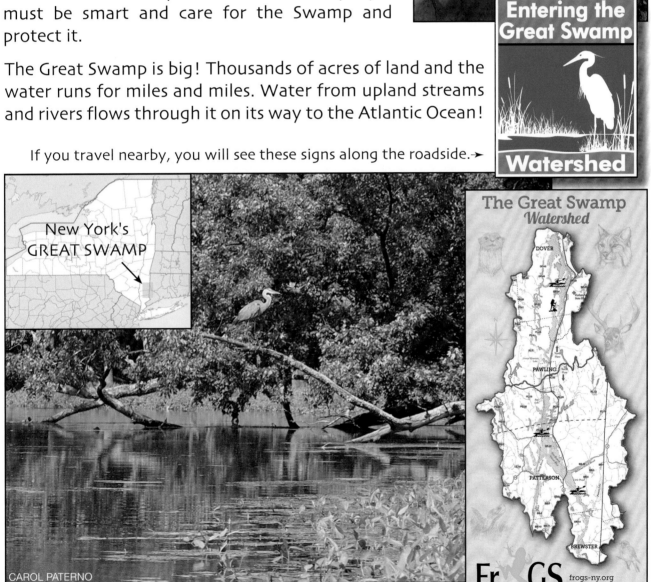

Entering the Great Swamp
Watershed

New York's GREAT SWAMP

The Great Swamp *Watershed*

DOVER

PAWLING

PATTERSON

BREWSTER

Fr GS
Friends of the Great Swamp
frogs-ny.org
info@frogs-ny.org
FrOGS-NY

CAROL PATERNO

A Great Blue Heron waits for its lunch to swim by.

Painted Turtles sun themselves on a log in the Great Swamp.

The water in the Swamp *does* flow in two directions! Because of a little hill in the middle, one part flows north and then east and on to the ocean. The other flows south into "reservoirs" (special "watershed" lakes) then into pipes to bring clean water all the way to New York City.

Deep in the Great Swamp you can hear only nature. It's very peaceful.

But the Great Swamp is so much more than that! It acts as a big green highway where wildlife can safely travel in the middle of our roads, houses and towns. Its wet meadows, ponds and streams are "habitats" (homes) for plants and animals including "rare" ones (that means there are so few left of their kind!) like the Bog Turtle. Some plants and animals *only* live in swamps.

Frogs live and *do* sing in the Swamp! Many animals live there or travel through in spring and fall. Some

Humbert? Is that you?

you may see if you visit: Otters who slide down the banks to fish the rivers. Beavers hard at work building dams that help protect their "lodge" homes. You might spy a black bear strolling by or spot the tracks of fox, bobcat or coyote.

Otters are playful and good swimmers!

You'd see and hear lots of birds as well: Swallows racing along the water catching insects. The Great Blue Heron waiting patiently for its lunch to swim by. Or the hoot of owls after the sun sets. Wood ducks nest in the tree tops to have their babies. Have you ever seen a duck in a tree? You can in the Great Swamp! Insects, dragonflies, and butterflies also call the Swamp home.

A female wood duck up a tree!

Red and silver Maple trees shade the waterway. Water lilies, purple-flowered Pickerel weed, fuzzy lizard's tails, and blue iris are some of the plants that grow in the very wet Swamp.

People hike parts of the Great Swamp. You can go to Pine Island. There's even a long boardwalk on one trail so you can cross the Swamp River. You can paddle its waters, or can ski or snow-shoe over the ice-covered river in winter.

Many people enjoy the Swamp: bird-watchers,

Purple-flowered Pickerel weed.

The Barred Owl hoots, "*Who cooks for you!*"

Swallows can be seen flying along the water hunting insects.

Look! It's our authors Carol (left) and Doris kayaking in the Great Swamp.

photographers, artists, hunters, boaters, and more. Others are studying it: students and teachers and scientists are learning more things about it all the time.

Because people need clean water to live, and many plants and wildlife need this habitat to survive, it is *very* important to keep the Great Swamp and the land around it as clean as possible.

A group of people joined together to help protect the Great Swamp. They study it and learn and then teach people about its beauty and its importance to our health, our state, and our world. This group is called FrOGS (how cool is that?), and it stands for <u>Fr</u>iends <u>o</u>f the <u>G</u>reat <u>S</u>wamp. These people work for *free* year round to keep the Swamp healthy and to teach us how we can *all* do our part to help keep the water and land clean in the Swamp (or wherever we live). You can be swamp smart! If you would like to learn more, visit their website at **frogs-ny.org**

Artists and photographers love the Swamp. Look at all that beauty!

FrOGS
Friends of the Great Swamp

32